Dear Parent:

Congratulations! Your child is taking the first steps on an exciting journey. The destination? Independent reading!

STEP INTO READING® will help your child get there. The program offers books at five levels that accompany children from their first attempts at reading to reading success. Each step includes fun stories, fiction and nonfiction, and colorful art. There are also Step into Reading Sticker Books, Step into Reading Math Readers, and Step into Reading Phonics Readers— a complete literacy program with something to interest every child.

Learning to Read, Step by Step!

Ready to Read   Preschool–Kindergarten
• big type and easy words • rhyme and rhythm • picture clues
For children who know the alphabet and are eager to begin reading.

Reading with Help   Preschool–Grade 1
• basic vocabulary • short sentences • simple stories
For children who recognize familiar words and sound out new words with help.

Reading on Your Own   Grades 1–3
• engaging characters • easy-to-follow plots • popular topics
For children who are ready to read on their own.

Reading Paragraphs   Grades 2–3
• challenging vocabulary • short paragraphs • exciting stories
For newly independent readers who read simple sentences with confidence.

Ready for Chapters   Grades 2–4
• chapters • longer paragraphs • full-color art
For children who want to take the plunge into chapter books but still like colorful pictures.

STEP INTO READING® is designed to give every child a successful reading experience. The grade levels are only guides. Children can progress through the steps at their own speed, developing confidence in their reading, no matter what their grade.

Remember, a lifetime love of reading starts with a single step!

To Sophie, who, thankfully, was found!
—C.P.M.

BARBIE and associated trademarks are owned by and used under license from Mattel, Inc.
© 2002 Mattel, Inc. All rights reserved under International and Pan-American Copyright
Conventions. Published in the United States by Random House Children's Books, a division of
Random House, Inc., New York, and simultaneously in Canada by Random House of Canada
Limited, Toronto. Originally published by Golden Books, an imprint of Random House
Children's Books, a division of Random House, Inc., in 2002.

www.stepintoreading.com

Educators and librarians, for a variety of teaching tools, visit us at
www.randomhouse.com/teachers

Library of Congress Cataloging-in-Publication Data
Pugliano-Martin, Carol.
Barbie : lost and found / by Carol Pugliano-Martin ; illustrated by S.I. International.   p.   cm.
— (Step into reading. A step 2 book)   SUMMARY: A lost puppy follows Stacie home, and with
Barbie's help she tries to find the owner.
ISBN 0-307-26219-7 (trade) — ISBN 0-307-46219-6 (lib. bdg.)
[1. Dolls—Fiction.   2. Dogs—Fiction.]
I. Title: Lost and found.   II. Title.   III. Series: Step into reading. Step 2 book.   PZ7.P953   Bar
2003   [E]—dc21   2002013655

Printed in the United States of America   13 12 11 10 9 8 7 6 5 4 3

First Random House Edition
STEP INTO READING, RANDOM HOUSE, and the Random House colophon are registered trademarks
of Random House, Inc.

Barbie
Lost and Found

By Carol Pugliano-Martin

Illustrated by S.I. International

Random House 🏠 New York

Barbie was reading
in her room.
All of a sudden, she heard
Stacie calling from outside.

"Barbie! Come quick!"
cried Stacie.

Barbie ran outside.
"Look who followed me home,"
said Stacie.
"Can I keep her?"

Barbie knelt down
to pet the dog.
She let the dog lick her hand.

"I don't see a collar or a tag," Barbie said.

"Does that mean I *can* keep her?" asked Stacie.

"Stacie, this dog might
belong to someone.
We have to find her owners,"
said Barbie.

"I guess you're right,"
said Stacie.
"Let's look for clues!"

"Well, she's all wet and muddy," said Barbie.

"Yes! That's the first clue!"
Stacie said.

She ran inside and got a notepad.
She wrote the clue on the pad.

"Now where could she have gotten so wet and muddy?" asked Barbie.

"There's a stream in the park,"
said Stacie.
They began walking.
The dog trotted beside them.

They came to the park.

The dog ran ahead.

"Barbie, she's heading right
to the stream," said Stacie.

When they got there,
the dog was standing
at the edge.
She was barking.

"This must be where
she got wet!" said Stacie.
"Do you like to swim, girl?"
The dog gave Stacie her paw.

19

"Look, Barbie," said Stacie.
"There's a branch in her fur.
It's another clue!"

Stacie wrote down the clue.
"Now we have to find
the bush it came from,"
she said.
They began to search the park.

"There it is!" cried Stacie.

They ran to the bush.

They saw something shiny.

It was a collar with a tag.

"The collar must have gotten
stuck here," said Barbie.
"Is your name Sophie?"
she asked the dog.
Sophie wagged her tail.

"The tag says Sophie
belongs to Mrs. Martin
on Oak Street," said Barbie.

They walked to the house.
Stacie rang the doorbell.

Mrs. Martin opened the door.
"Hi, I'm Stacie.
My sister, Barbie, and I think
we found your dog."

"She followed me home,"
said Stacie.
"I found clues and
we brought her here."

"Thank you!" said Mrs. Martin.
"You should be a detective
when you grow up.
You would be a great one!"

"I would like to work
at an animal shelter instead.
I want to help animals
find homes," said Stacie.

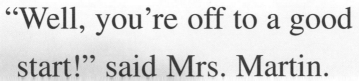
"Well, you're off to a good start!" said Mrs. Martin.

"Woof!" Sophie agreed.